The Tale of Sir Spiffing Biffing

Maureen Haselhurst
Illustrated by Chris Mould

Chapter 1

Sir Spiffing Biffing longed to be a bold, brave knight.

He had been to Knight School, but he wasn't very good at sword-swishing. Climbing tall towers made him dizzy and splatting dragons was so messy!

Besides, he still got the goodies and the baddies mixed up.

When other knights rode past, the people cheered.
When Sir Spiffing Biffing rode past, the people
laughed.

"Yoo-hoo! Sir Cowardy-Custard!" they called.

Sir Spiffing Biffing didn't like being called names.
But he wasn't brave enough to do anything about it.

So one morning, Sir Spiffing Biffing set out to find adventure. As he rode, he sang to himself,
*"I'm Sir Spiffing Biffing. I like a little song.
I biff goodies and I put rights wrong."*
"No, no, no," snorted his horse, Humphrey. "You biff baddies and you put wrongs right."
"Do I?" said Sir Spiff, and he rode on.

He went to see his friend, Princess Pammy. She was climbing down a rope from her bedroom window.

"Just in time," she said. "You can help me."

"Sorry, I don't like heights," said Sir Spiff. "Must dash!"

He rode off slowly. Galloping made him feel sick.

"There'll be an easy adventure just round the corner," said Humphrey.

And there was . . .

Sir Spiffing Biffing came across a large, iron cage. An old man and a strange animal were locked inside.

"Help!" cried the old man when he saw the knight.

Sir Spiffing Biffing walked bravely up to the cage.

"Are you a goodie or a baddie?" he said in his boldest voice.

The man grinned.

"I am the goodiest goodie in the land, and this is my pet, Diddums," he said. "We were locked in this cage by Baron Beastly. Please help us, brave knight."

"Right you are!" said Sir Spiff.

He swished at the lock with his sword. On the
fourth swish, the lock broke and the door opened.

The old man and his pet burst from the cage.
There was a rush and a roar and a sizzle of sparks
and suddenly . . .

"A DRAGON!" yelled Humphrey.

"Ha! Ha! Foolish knight!" bellowed the man.
"I am Baron Beastly, the baddiest baddie in the land!
And you have set me free."

He leapt onto his dragon and off they flew.

"Oops!" said Sir Spiffing Biffing, and he rode on.

Soon he came to a very tall tower. Someone was waving wildly from the window. It was Princess Pammy.

"Help!" she yelled. "I've been locked in here by Baron Beastly."

Sir Spiffing Biffing looked up. He felt dizzy.

"Can't you get down yourself?" he shouted.

"No!" snapped Princess Pammy. "You have to rescue me. But not in that tatty old armour. Princesses are rescued by knights in **shining** armour."

"Right you are!" called Sir Spiff, trying to sound brave.

"Bossy boots!" muttered Humphrey.

Chapter 2

Sir Spiffing Biffing went home and emptied his piggy bank. He had three bent buttons.

He put them in his pocket and went off to a cart-boot sale. He saw lots of suits of armour. Then, something very shiny caught his eye. It had springs on its feet and long arms for plucking princesses out of towers. It was perfect!

"I wonder how much it costs," said Sir Spiff.

"Three bent buttons," said the armour. "I'm on special offer."

"Wow! It talks!" cried Sir Spiff.

"Of course. I'm a Hornswoggle."

"A what?" asked Sir Spiff.

"I'm a sort of robot knight," boasted the Hornswoggle. "I can do all that baddie biffing and dragon splatting for you. Now are you going to buy me, or not?"

"You bet!" cried Sir Spiff and handed over his buttons.

Sir Spiffing Biffing and the Hornswoggle rode off to rescue Princess Pammy.

The Hornswoggle was a terrible show-off. Wherever there was a wrong to right or a baddie to biff, the Hornswoggle would do it. Sir Spiffing Biffing hid behind a bush.

"This is great!" he chuckled. "Everyone thinks I'm a bold, brave knight!"

"It's cheating," snorted Humphrey.

By the time they got to the tall tower, the sky was
getting darker and darker. It started to rain.

"Wow! Love the armour!" shouted Princess Pammy.
The Hornswoggle strutted around proudly.

But something was wrong. The Hornswoggle stopped moving.

"I'm rusting!" it creaked, and it fell down like a pile of scrap metal.

Princess Pammy spotted Sir Spiffing Biffing hiding behind a bush.

"You big cheat!" she yelled.

"Yes, what a no-good, cowardy-custard," someone snarled behind him. It was Baron Beastly.

Sir Spiffing Biffing rushed out of the bushes. His face was as red as a cherry. He looked VERY angry.

"Don't you dare call me names, you beastly baddie," he yelled.

He swished his sword angrily and it crashed into the Hornswoggle. A piece of rusted robot flew into the air. It landed with a thump on Baron Beastly's head.

"Well done, Spiffy!" shouted Princess Pammy.
Sir Spiffing Biffing looked up at the tall tower.
For a moment he felt dizzy.

"Oh, get on with it," snorted Humphrey, and he
kicked Sir Spiff high into the air.

Up, up, up he shot and he plucked Princess
Pammy from her window.

Then down, down, down they came and they landed with a thump on something large and lumpy. It was Diddums!

"Wow, Spiffy!" said Princess Pammy. "You're a
very bold, brave knight."

"Yes, I am!" cried Sir Spiff. "I really biffed that
baddie. I really splatted that dragon. Yippee!"

He leapt onto his horse and proudly sang:
"I'm Sir Spiffing Biffing, the bold, brave knight.
I biff baddies and I put wrongs right."

"At last!" snorted Humphrey, and off they galloped
to find more adventures.